I0746726

DAME WIGGINS OF LEE

DAME WIGGINS
OF LEE,

AND HER

SEVEN WONDERFUL CATS.

A HUMOROUS TALE.

BY A LADY OF NINETY

EMBELLISHED WITH NINETEEN NEATLY COLOURED ENGRAVINGS.

Dame Wiggins of Lee
		Was a worthy old soul,
As e'er threaded a nee-dle,
		Or wash in a bowl;

She held mice and rats
		In such antipathy,
That seven fine cats,
		Kept Dame Wiggins of Lee.

KINDNESS

Seven fine cats

Kept Dame Wiggins of Lee.

The rats and mice scared
    By this fierce whiskered crew,
The poor seven cats
    Soon had nothing to do;

So, as any one idle,
    She ne'er loved to see,
She sent them to school,
    Did Dame Wiggins of Lee.

EDUCATION

She sent them to school,

Did Dame Wiggins of Lee.

But soon she grew tired,
  Of living alone,
So she sent for her cats,
  From school to come home;

Each rowing a wherry,
  Returning you see;
The frolic made merry
  Dame Wiggins of Lee.

RETURN HOME

Each rowing a wherry,

Returning you see;

The Dame was quite pleased,
　　And ran out to market,
When she came back
　　They were mending the carpet.

The needle each handled
　　As brisk as a bee:
"Well done, my good cats,"
　　Said Dame Wiggins of Lee.

MENDING

When she came back,

They were mending the carpet.

To give them a treat,
    She ran out for some rice;
When she came back,
    They were skating on ice;

"I shall soon see one down,
    Aye, perhaps, two or three,
I'll bet half-a-crown,"
    Said Dame Wiggins of Lee.

SKATING

When she came back,

They were skating on ice.

While, to make a nice pudding,
　　She went for a sparrow,
They were wheeling a sick lamb,
　　Home in a wheel-barrow.

"You shall all have some sprats,
　　For your humanity,
My seven good cats,"
　　Said Dame Wiggins of Lee.

HUMANITY

Bringing a sick lamb,

Home in a wheel-barrow.

While she ran to the field,
  To look for its dam,
They were warming the bed
  For the poor sick lamb;

They turned up the clothes,
  As neat as could be;
"I shall ne'er want a nurse,"
  Said Dame Wiggins of Lee.

CARE

Warming the bed
For the poor sick lamb.

She wished them good night,
    And went up to bed;
When lo! in the morning,
    The cats were all fled.

But soon, what a fuss!
    "Where can they all be?
Here, pussy, puss, puss!"
    Cried Dame Wiggins of Lee.

CONCERN

Lo! in the morning,

The cats were all fled.

Her heart was nigh broke,
    So she sat down to weep;
When she saw them come back,
    Each riding a sheep.

She fondled and patted,
    Each purring Tom-my:
"Ah! Welcome my dears,"
    Said Dame Wiggins of Lee.

GRIEF

She saw them come back,

Each riding a sheep.

The Dame was unable,
　　Her pleasure to smother,
To see the sick lamb,
　　Jump up to his mother;

In spite of the gout,
　　And a pain in her knee,
She went dancing about;
　　Did Dame Wiggins of Lee.

PLEASURE

She went dancing about,

Did Dame Wiggins of Lee.

The Farmer soon heard,
    Where his sheep went astray,
And arrived at Dame's door,
    With his faithful dog Tray.

He knocked with his crook,
    When, the stranger to see,
Out of window did look,
    Dame Wiggins of Lee.

ENQUIRY

Out of window did look

Dame Wiggins of Lee.

For their kindness he had them,
    All drawn by his team,
He gave them some field-mice,
    With raspberry cream;

Said he, "All my farm,
    You shall presently see;
For I honour the cats,
    Of Dame Wiggins of Lee.'

THE RIDE

For their kindness he had them

All drawn by his team.

He sent his maid out
    For some muffins and crumpets;
And when he turn'd round
    They were blowing of trumpets.

Said he, "I suppose,
    She's as deaf as can be,
Or this ne'er could be borne
    By Dame Wiggins of Lee."

THE RIDE

And when he turn'd round

They were blowing of trumpets.

To show them his poultry,
　　He turned them all loose;
When each nimbly leaped
　　On the back of a goose;

Which frightened them so,
　　That they ran to the sea,
And half drowned the poor cats
　　Of Dame Wiggins of Lee

FRIGHT

Which frightened them so,

That they ran to the sea.

For the care of his Lamb,
    And their comical pranks,
He gave them a ham,
    With abundance of thanks.

"I wish you good day,
    My fine fellows," said he:
"My compliments, pray,
    To Dame Wiggins of Lee."

GRATITUDE

He gave them a ham,

With abundance of thanks.

You see them arrived
     At the Dame's welcome door;
They show her their presents,
     With all their good store.

"Now come in to supper,
     And sit down with me,
Right welcome, one more,"
     Said Dame Wiggins of Lee.

THE FEAST

Now come in to supper,

And sit down with me.

This edition published 2024
by Living Book Press
Copyright © Living Book Press, 2024

ISBN: 978-1-76153-580-2 (softcover)

First published in 1823.

All rights reserved. No part of this publication may be reproduced, stored in a retrieval system, or transmitted in any other form or means – electronic, mechanical, photocopying, recording or otherwise, without the prior permission of the copyright owner and the publisher or as provided by Australian law.

A catalogue record for this book is available from the National Library of Australia

www.ingramcontent.com/pod-product-compliance
Lightning Source LLC
Chambersburg PA
CBHW042112160726
48295CB00018B/1077